# Look at Lucy!

by Ilene Cooper
illustrated by David Merrell

A STEPPING STONE BOOK™
Random House New York

This is a work of fiction. Names, characters, places, and incidents either are the product of the author's imagination or are used fictitiously. Any resemblance to actual persons, living or dead, events, or locales is entirely coincidental.



www.steppingstonesbooks.com
www.randomhouse.com/kids

Educators and librarians, for a variety of teaching tools, visit us at
www.randomhouse.com/teachers

*Library of Congress Cataloging-in-Publication Data*
Cooper, Ilene.
Look at Lucy! / by Ilene Cooper ; illustrated by David Merrell. — 1st ed.
p. cm.
"A Stepping Stone Book."
Summary: Entering his beagle, Lucy, in a contest to be "spokespet" for Pet-O-Rama helps shy, nine-year-old Bobby get over his anxiety about speaking in front of groups of people, from his third-grade classmates to the contest judges.
ISBN 978-0-375-85558-0 (pbk.) — ISBN 978-0-375-95558-7 (lib. bdg.)
[1. Bashfulness—Fiction. 2. Anxiety—Fiction. 3. Contests—Fiction. 4. Schools—Fiction. 5. Beagle (Dog breed)—Fiction. 6. Dogs—Fiction.]
I. Merrell, David Webber, ill. II. Title.
PZ7.C7856Loo 2009 [E]—dc22 2008036312

Printed in the United States of America
10 9 8 7 6 5 4 3 2
First Edition
Random House Children's Books supports the First Amendment and celebrates the right to read.

*With great thanks to Jennifer Arena—*
*who loves Lucy almost as much as I do.*
*—I.C.*

*To our beloved dog, Mary*
*—D.M.*

# Contents

# School Blues

Bobby Quinn sat on the front steps of his house. He watched one tired leaf float down from the big oak tree in the yard.

"Uh-oh," said Bobby. Falling leaves. Okay, one leaf. But many more were sure to follow. Bobby knew what that meant. School would start soon.

School. Bobby didn't want to think about school.

And for just that moment he didn't have to. A bark came from behind the screen door. It was Lucy. Lucy was a brown and white beagle with black spots and eyes the color of chocolate kisses.

Bobby's parents had given Lucy to him for his eighth birthday, earlier in the summer. She was absolutely the best dog ever! *Absolutely* was Bobby's favorite word.

"*A-hooo! A-hooo!*" Lucy's bark turned into a howl. A howl meant she wanted out of the house, and she wanted out right now.

"Okay, girl," Bobby said with a smile. "You can come and sit with me."

But Lucy wasn't the kind of dog who liked to sit. She was the kind of dog who liked to run and jump. She liked to run so much that a few weeks ago she had run away. Bobby and his friend Shawn had to

chase her all around their town. For a few anxious moments, Bobby had been afraid he might not see Lucy again.

Just the thought of that day gave him a stomachache. Since then, Bobby hadn't taken any chances. He hurried to shut the gate before he let Lucy out of the house.

When Lucy was free, she leapt down the steps into the yard. Yipping and yapping, she stood next to the Frisbee that Bobby had dropped in the grass the day before. Lucy looked at Bobby with her big brown eyes. *Pick it up! Throw it!* That was what her barks seemed to say.

Bobby didn't have to be asked twice. He hurled the red Frisbee, and Lucy went on the chase. Bobby threw. Lucy chased. Every time Lucy brought back the Frisbee, she pranced around, waiting for the next toss.

School might be starting soon, but it was still summer, and it was hot. Bobby wondered where Lucy got all her energy. He wiped the sweat from his forehead.

"Hi, Bobby," a voice called.

Bobby looked up and saw his friend Shawn at the gate. Shawn had moved in across the street over the summer, and Lucy had brought the two shy boys together.

Bobby wasn't as shy as he used to be. But when he thought about school, he got nervous. He didn't really have any friends in his class. He had always been too shy to talk to the other kids. Would things be any better this year?

"Hey, Shawn. Come in," Bobby said.

Shawn opened the gate and carefully closed it behind him. Chasing Lucy all over town was still very clear in his mind, too.

He didn't want to go through that again.

Lucy ran over to Shawn and sniffed his hand. She dashed back to the Frisbee. She looked first at Bobby, then at Shawn. *Well? Let's play*, she seemed to say.

Instead Bobby said, "It's too hot, Lucy." He turned to Shawn. "Let's go inside and have some lemonade."

"Okay. I have something to tell you."

As Bobby and Shawn headed for the door, Lucy started barking again. She wasn't going to give up playtime that easily.

Sometimes Bobby gave in to Lucy's wishes, but not today. He opened the door wide. "Come in, Lucy."

What could a dog do? She dashed past the boys and led the way into the house.

Bobby went right to the refrigerator and opened it. The cold air hit him. It felt great. He grabbed the lemonade pitcher and brought it to the table. Then he took a couple of glasses off the counter and poured the lemonade.

"So what's up, Shawn?" he asked.

Shawn took a glass. "My parents said I could get a pet."

"A dog?" Bobby knew Shawn had wanted a dog for a long time.

Shawn shook his head. "No. They said I should start with something small."

"A hamster? A turtle? A bird?" Bobby asked.

Shawn shrugged. "I don't know. I haven't decided yet."

Mrs. Quinn came into the kitchen. "Bobby," she said, "we need to go to the mall and pick up some things for school. And I need to stop at Pet-O-Rama and buy some food for Lucy."

*School.* There was that word again. Then he had a thought. "Can Shawn come with us, Mom? He's looking for a pet," Bobby informed his mother. "He doesn't know what kind yet. A trip to Pet-O-Rama will give him some ideas."

"Okay. We're leaving in a few minutes. I'll call your mother, Shawn, and make sure it's fine for you to come with us," Bobby's mother said.

Shawn nodded. Like Bobby, he didn't find it easy to speak up.

Bobby looked at Shawn. *Is Shawn worried about school starting, too?* Bobby wondered.

It was hard to be the new kid. But in a way, Bobby wished he could be the new kid. He would like a fresh start. He was sure plenty of his classmates remembered that in kindergarten he was so shy, he used to cry. His nickname was Cry Bobby.

"Shawn . . . ," Bobby began.

"What?"

"School is starting soon."

"I know," Shawn answered quietly. "How could I forget?"

From the look on Shawn's face, Bobby had his answer. Shawn wasn't any happier about school than he was.

# Pet-O-Rama

Pencils. Notebooks. Crayons. Bobby and his mother filled up a shopping cart with school supplies. Shawn's mother had said he should buy some things, too. So Shawn added his items to the cart.

"Mom, when will we find out if Shawn and I are in the same classroom?" Bobby asked.

"We should hear in the next few days,"

Mrs. Quinn said as she pushed the cart down the crowded aisles.

"I sure hope we're in the same room," Bobby told Shawn.

"Me too," Shawn answered. "At least you know some kids at school. I don't know anybody."

"You know Candy," Mrs. Quinn reminded Shawn. "She's in our school district now. She might be in your class."

Candy was a new friend Bobby had made in dog obedience class. Lucy wasn't a very good student, but Candy's dog, Butch, was terrible. He sat when he was told to stand. He sat when he was asked to fetch. Sometimes in the middle of class he just lay down and closed his eyes.

"It would be great if Candy ends up in our classroom," Bobby said. "She talks so much, we wouldn't have to talk at all."

The boys grinned at each other. They both liked Candy, but sometimes it was hard to get a word in edgewise.

*Shawn and Candy in his room.* Bobby wondered what it would be like to have two friends in class. Then his smile faded. What if they wanted Bobby to introduce them to the other kids? Bobby barely knew the boys and girls who had been with him in kindergarten, first grade, and second grade. Most of the kids ignored him.

Bobby started to feel funny. Maybe it wouldn't be so great to have Shawn and Candy as classmates. He didn't want them to know how unpopular he was.

"Bobby? You haven't heard a word I've said," his mother told him.

Bobby shrugged. It was true. He hadn't.

"I want to do a little clothes shopping," his mother repeated.

Bobby groaned.

"We'll get to the pet store soon," Mrs. Quinn said. She was already pushing her cart toward the kids' clothing section.

Bobby sighed. The best thing to do was to make clothes shopping go as fast as possible.

Bobby picked out a blue shirt. And a sweatshirt with a football helmet on it.

His mother put the clothes in the cart. "All right. Would you like to try on some jeans?"

Bobby and Shawn looked at each other. That could take forever.

Mrs. Quinn gave up. "I can see you're not in the mood to try on jeans right now."

*Right now?* Bobby thought. *I'll never be in the mood for that.*

"Let's check out," Mrs. Quinn said. "Then we'll go to the pet store."

"Finally," Bobby whispered to Shawn. Shawn just nodded.

But they weren't out of the store yet. There was a long checkout line, and it was moving slowly.

"Mom . . . ," Bobby pleaded.

"All right," Mrs. Quinn said. "Pet-O-Rama is right next door. Go to the pet section and meet me there. Stick together!"

"We will!" Bobby and Shawn couldn't get out of the store fast enough.

Pet-O-Rama was a big, brightly lit store. One half of it was packed with pet supplies. It had everything from dog food to kitty litter to mealworms. Once Bobby had picked up a container of the bugs and asked his dad what they were for.

"I think lizards eat them," his father had said.

Lizards. Bobby was glad he didn't have a lizard for a pet.

The other side of the store was much more interesting. That was where the animals were kept.

"Let's go over there," Bobby said to Shawn. He pointed in the direction of several large birdcages.

Bobby had never really spent much time on the pet side of Pet-O-Rama. As they walked up and down the aisles, he was surprised by how many choices there were.

"Do you want a bird?" Bobby asked.

They stopped in front of several large glass cases full of birds. There were parakeets in different shades of blue and green. Small songbirds chirped away. In a corner cage, standing proudly on his perch, was a big, colorful parrot.

"I wouldn't know which one to pick," Shawn said.

The boys were drawn to a glass-walled room with some cages on tall shelves. Inside the cages, several cats roamed. One black cat batted a toy mouse back and forth. A fluffy white cat nibbled on some dry food. And two kittens tussled with each other in a corner of one of the cages.

"Can you have a cat?" Bobby asked.

Shawn shook his head. "My sister is allergic to cat hair," he explained.

"Too bad." If Bobby didn't have Lucy, he might like to own a cat.

"My mom said I should look at small pets," Shawn said.

So the boys checked out the hamsters, guinea pigs, and turtles. Shawn seemed a little dazed. "So many choices," he murmured. He almost seemed relieved when Mrs. Quinn came up to the boys.

"Have you made any decisions?" she asked Shawn.

He shook his head.

"Well, think about it." Mrs. Quinn looked at her watch. "Let's go buy Lucy's food and get home."

On the way out, a large, colorful poster taller than the boys caught Bobby's eye.

The poster had a drawing of different kinds of animals crowded together in front of a television camera. Across the top were the words WANTED: SPOKESPET FOR PET-O-RAMA! Under the picture of the animals it said, "Is your pet cute? Smart? Funny? Enter the Pet-O-Rama spokespet contest and your pet could be on TV!"

Bobby read the poster carefully. Cute, smart, funny? That described Lucy! She could win the spokespet contest, easy!

# Spokespet

Big news! Bobby heard all kinds of big news on Friday.

First, a letter came in the mail. In the corner of the envelope it said, "Wildwood Elementary School."

"Does it say what room I'm going to be in?" Bobby asked with excitement.

"Let's see." Mrs. Quinn sat down at the kitchen table and opened the letter. Bobby sat next to her. Lucy joined them. She stretched up, putting her front paws on Bobby's knees. Her head strained toward the table. She wanted to hear the big news.

"You're in Mrs. Lee's room," Bobby's mother told him.

"Yeah!" Bobby said. Shawn had gotten his letter yesterday. He was in Mrs. Lee's room, too.

*"Woof!"* Lucy barked. *"Woof!"* Then she scooted off.

Bobby laughed. "Lucy must know that Mrs. Lee is the teacher I wanted."

"I've heard she's very good," Mrs. Quinn said. She read the rest of the letter. "I see there are a few more supplies to pick up. We'll have to go back to the mall. We can do a little more clothes shopping."

Bobby groaned. He thought he was done

with shopping. What was next? New underwear? Then Bobby had a thought. There was a good reason to go to the mall. He could go to Pet-O-Rama and get an entry form for the contest.

"When can we go?" Bobby asked.

Mrs. Quinn looked at Bobby with surprise. "How about right now?" she asked.

"First I have to call Shawn," Bobby said. Shawn wasn't home. So he left a message. "I'm in Mrs. Lee's room, too!"

At the mall Bobby suffered through trying on new shoes. But he came home with the prize—the entry form for the Pet-O-Rama contest.

The next big news came from Shawn. That afternoon, he came over to Bobby's house with a big smile on his face and something behind his back.

"Did you get my message?" Bobby asked.

"Yep." He and Bobby high-fived. "And I got something else, too," said Shawn. He pulled a small wire cage from behind his back.

At first Bobby didn't see anything in the cage. Then he looked more closely. Huddled under a pile of shredded newspapers was a small, furry body with a long, long tail. "A mouse?" Bobby asked.

"Yep," said a pleased Shawn. "A mouse."

Bobby was surprised. They had looked at lots of animals at Pet-O-Rama, but no mice.

Shawn laughed. "I know. I didn't think I was going to get a mouse, either. But when I went back to Pet-O-Rama, I saw a glass cage with a couple of mice in it. I knocked on it, and this guy came right to me. It was like he was saying, 'Take me home.' So I did."

"He's white," Bobby said. He thought mice were brown.

"Yep, a white mouse with a pink nose and a pink tail."

"And tiny paws," Bobby said. "What's his name?"

"Twitch. Because of the way he twitches his whiskers," Shawn replied.

Bobby put his finger up to the wire cage. Sure enough, the little white mouse twitched his long whiskers before giving Bobby a sniff.

Last autumn several mice had made a home under the kitchen sink. One day, Mrs. Quinn opened the door, and four brown mice came running out. Bobby's mother had let out a shriek that could compete with one of Lucy's howls. She wouldn't go back in the kitchen until Bobby's father swore he had caught them all in a shoe box. Mr. Quinn had let them go in the empty lot down the street.

"Twitch is kind of cute," Bobby admitted.

"Mice are great," Shawn told him. "Think of all the great mice in history. There's Mickey Mouse, Mighty Mouse, the Mouse and the Motorcycle."

Bobby was catching some of Shawn's excitement. "Maybe we could buy Twitch a toy motorcycle."

"Or build him a house. A mouse house," Shawn said.

Bobby was glad he had a dog for a pet, but playing with a mouse might be fun, too.

Just then, the last bit of news came in with a bang. Candy came bursting in the door. Her dog, Butch, was right on her heels.

"Hey, did you hear? I'm in Mrs. Lee's room, too!" she said.

Bobby was about to say, "Cool," but Candy plowed on. "At first I was mad when my mom told us we were moving, even though it was just a couple of blocks away. 'Cause I had to change schools and go to Wildwood. I was pretty sure I wouldn't like Wildwood. No friends. But now I know you guys, and you're my friends, right? And it turns out I'm going to be in your room, which is good. Mrs. Lee is nice, right?"

"Right," Shawn said quickly before Candy could get started again.

Lucy bounded up from the basement, where she had followed a ball that had bounced down the stairs. She didn't notice Twitch, but when she saw Butch she gave a sharp bark. Butch barked right back. Lucy offered up a howl.

Shawn put Twitch's cage on the patio table. Candy stuck her face close to the cage. "A mouse, huh?"

"His name is Twitch," Shawn told her.

"Twitch, that's cute. 'Cause of the whiskers, I bet," Candy said. "I'm not much for rodents. Mice are rodents, you know. So are rats, and hamsters, and guinea pigs—"

"Yeah, they are," Bobby agreed. He hoped Candy didn't know any more rodents.

"And gerbils. Gerbils are rodents, too. Maybe chinchillas. I'm not sure," Candy told the boys. "Well, I've never been a big fan of rodents. But Twitch might change my mind. White's a nice color, for a mouse, and that little pink nose—"

Shawn interrupted Candy. "Twitch is so fine, I'm going to enter him in a contest."

"What contest?" Candy asked.

"It's a contest they're having at Pet-O-Rama," Shawn explained.

"The spokespet contest?" Bobby asked.

Candy looked confused. "A spokespet? Is that even a word? What's a spokespet?"

Bobby laughed. It was a funny word. A funny idea, too, he guessed. "Well, you've heard of a spokesperson?" he asked.

"Yeah," Candy answered. "Like when a company has a movie star or somebody famous do their commercials."

"Right," Bobby said. "Well, Pet-O-Rama doesn't want a person in their commercials. They want a pet."

"Uh, news flash. Pets can't talk," Candy said.

Bobby pulled the contest entry form from his pocket. " 'The winning pet from this store will move on to the regional contest,' " he read. " 'The winner of that contest will be featured in print and television ads.' " Bobby looked up. "See, the winner doesn't have to talk. She just has to look good for the cameras."

Shawn pulled an entry form from his own pocket. "I picked this up when I bought Twitch. I guess Lucy and Twitch will both be in the contest."

"What about Butch?" Candy asked. "I'll enter him in the contest, too. Butch would make a great spokespet!"

Out in the yard, Lucy was trying to get Butch to play. But Butch was on his back, staring up at the sky. He gave himself a hard scratch. Then he rolled over, closed his eyes, and went to sleep.

Bobby figured there'd be lots of pets in the contest. Lucy would have plenty of competition. But he didn't think he had to worry much about Butch.

# Mrs. Lee's Room

There was a funny feeling in the pit of Bobby's stomach. And it wasn't a ha-ha funny feeling. It was a weird, unsettled feeling. It had been there since he got out of bed.

Bobby put on the new clothes his mother had laid out for him the night before and went downstairs. He knew she would want him to eat, but breakfast seemed like a bad idea.

Lucy was waiting for him at the bottom of the stairs. She wasn't her usual bouncy self. Maybe she knew it was the first day of school, too.

Mr. and Mrs. Quinn were drinking coffee at the table. Bobby's mother had made his favorite, pancakes. He wished he felt like eating.

"Hey, Bobby," his father said. He looked over the top of his newspaper. "You're a third grader. How does it feel?"

"Not too good," Bobby told him. "I'm not hungry, Mom. I don't feel well."

Mrs. Quinn touched her hand to Bobby's forehead. "You don't have a fever. I think you might be nervous about school, that's all," she said.

Bobby nodded. He picked up Lucy and put her on his lap. Lucy licked Bobby's cheek.

"Well, it will be a big change for both of you," his mother said. "Just remember, Lucy and I will be waiting here when you come home at three o'clock."

Bobby thought three o'clock seemed like a long way off.

Since his mother insisted, Bobby ate a few bites of his pancakes and drank some of his milk. Lucy sat on his lap the whole time. Usually his mother wouldn't have allowed that, but she looked like she felt sorry for both of them.

After breakfast, Bobby gave Lucy a kiss on the top of her head. Finally he told his father, "I'm ready." Wildwood School was close enough to walk to, but today Bobby's father was going to drive him and Shawn.

When Shawn got in the car, he was just as quiet as Bobby. Mr. Quinn looked at them in the rearview mirror. "I think you boys are going to have a great year!" he said.

Bobby nodded, and Shawn said, "Yes, sir." Bobby hoped his father was right.

Mr. Quinn dropped them off in front of Wildwood. The schoolyard was full of kids laughing and talking. Bobby walked slowly toward the school. Shawn was right beside him.

"Do you know any of these kids?" Shawn asked.

Bobby spotted a few boys and girls from his class last year. He sure didn't feel like going up to them and saying hi. What if they didn't remember him? What if they did remember him and thought he was a dope? "Uh . . ."

Just then, Shawn and Bobby heard a familiar voice. "Hi, guys!"

Candy came hurrying up to them. Her smile was almost as bright as the stars on her shiny blue backpack.

"Hey, this seems okay," she said, looking around. "Good playground, lots of kids. Who's in our class?"

Bobby hesitated, but Candy was waiting. He pointed to the kids he had spotted before. "There's Carrie, Dexter, Jessie, and Robin. They might be in Mrs. Lee's room with us," he mumbled.

Candy gave Bobby a funny look. "Let's go say hi."

"Aw, I don't feel like it right now," Bobby protested.

But Candy wasn't the kind of girl who took no for an answer. And she certainly was not shy. "Come on," she said to Bobby and Shawn.

Keeping a few steps behind her, Bobby and Shawn watched Candy walk up to Carrie, Dexter, Jessie, and Robin. "Hello, I'm Candy. I'm new this year," she said.

At first the four kids seemed surprised. Then Candy started asking them what Wildwood was like. For once, she let other people talk, too. Soon everyone was eager to tell her about Wildwood School.

"Hey, Bobby, Shawn," Candy said, calling them over. "You know Bobby, right?" she asked her new friends. "He was in your grade last year. You don't know Shawn, though. He just moved here this summer."

"Where did you come from?" Jessie asked.

In a soft voice, Shawn said, "Chicago."

Bobby was worried that no one had heard Shawn, but Dexter said, "My grandma lives in Chicago. We visited her in July."

That broke the ice. Shawn and Dexter started talking about Chicago. They both liked the Chicago Cubs.

Bobby felt a little jealous. He liked the Cubs as much as Shawn did. He wanted to join the conversation, too. He just didn't know how.

Then Robin turned to him. "What did you do over the summer, Bobby?"

"I . . . I got a dog," Bobby said.

"Yeah? What kind?" Robin seemed interested.

Before Bobby could answer, the first bell rang. Everyone began hurrying toward the big double doors. "I know where our room is," Bobby told Candy and Shawn. "Follow me."

Room 102 was down a long hall. "That's the learning center." Bobby pointed it out. "And the gym is back there."

When they got to Room 102, they chose three seats together near the windows. Bobby liked looking outside if things got boring.

However, it didn't look like Mrs. Lee's class was going to be boring. After they said the Pledge of Allegiance, Mrs. Lee took attendance. Then she talked about all the interesting things she had planned for the

MRS.

year. They were going to learn about the pioneers and visit a real-life pioneer cabin. In math class, they'd be spending time on long division.

When Jessie called out, "Long division is hard," Mrs. Lee laughed.

"You'll like it, you'll see," she said. She also listed some of the books she was going to read aloud. One was *The Mouse and the Motorcycle*!

"Wait until she finds out you have a mouse," Bobby whispered to Shawn.

"Maybe we'll have a motorcycle for Twitch by then. We'll bring him to school," Shawn whispered back.

Pretty much everything Mrs. Lee described for the coming year sounded fine to Bobby. Maybe his father was right. Maybe this was going to be a good year. Then Mrs.

Lee said something that made Bobby's heart beat faster. Something that didn't sound good at all.

"One more thing. We're going to be doing lots of oral reports. We'll report on books we've read, and the work we're doing. I think sharing with your classmates will be lots of fun, don't you?"

Standing up, talking in front of twenty-five kids? Bobby had trouble telling Robin he had gotten a dog this summer. How in the world could he give an oral report? Lots of oral reports.

*No, Mrs. Lee, oral reports will not be fun,* Bobby thought. *Absolutely not.*

# Troubles

There were some things Bobby liked about school. He liked Mrs. Lee. He liked having Shawn and Candy in his class. He liked listening to *The Mouse and the Motorcycle.*

Lucy didn't like anything about Bobby spending the day at school. Mrs. Quinn said she moped around the house while Bobby was gone. When he came home, Lucy went crazy. She barked. She ran around in circles.

She grabbed shoes, magazines, and clothes and chewed them. She hadn't done that in weeks. One day, Bobby came home from school and found Lucy chomping on one of his best sneakers.

"Hey, Lucy! Quit that!" Bobby ran over to her. He tried to pull the blue sneaker from Lucy's mouth.

Lucy pulled right back. It was a tug-of-war. Finally Lucy let the shoe drop. It was too late. Bobby stuck his finger through a big hole near the toe.

"What are we going to do about Lucy?" Mrs. Quinn fretted.

"Bobby, you have to walk her as soon as you get home from school," his father told him that night. "Exercise will help her get rid of some of that energy."

Bobby was happy to walk Lucy every day. She pranced around the neighborhood. In the yard, she caught sticks and balls when Bobby threw them. She let off lots of extra steam. If Lucy was in a cartoon, she'd have steam coming out from under her long, floppy ears.

But she still liked to chew shoes.

Bobby had been in school for about two

weeks when Mrs. Lee made an announcement. "Class, it's time to start thinking about our oral reports," she said.

*Uh-oh,* Bobby thought. He had hoped Mrs. Lee had forgotten about those stupid oral reports. He glanced over at Shawn. Shawn looked like he had just swallowed a hot pepper.

"For the first report," Mrs. Lee went on, "I want you to talk about a very special subject. You."

Bobby was surprised. He thought Mrs. Lee would want the class to give reports about history. They were studying the Pilgrims. They were learning about the Native Americans who were already living in this country when the Pilgrims got here. Wasn't that the kind of thing reports were about?

Mrs. Lee explained. "I think it will be fun

if everyone gets up and speaks for a few minutes. Introduce yourself to the class. Tell us a little about your family, your pets, your hobbies. Just get up and talk."

*Just get up and talk?* Bobby thought. Just jumping out of an airplane might be easier for him.

Some kids raised their hands. Mrs. Lee called on Dexter.

"Can we read our reports?" he asked.

"Maybe later in the year. Then the reports will be longer. They'll have more facts in them," Mrs. Lee answered. "I don't think you'll need any notes for this one. It will be easy. You don't need to write down the names of your brothers and sisters, do you?"

Bobby was glad he didn't have any brothers or sisters. Their names would be one more thing to remember.

Candy was waving her hand.

"Yes, Candy," Mrs. Lee said.

"Will you give a report about yourself, Mrs. Lee? Since we're all finding out about each other, I want to learn some things about you. Like are you married? Well, I guess you are 'cause your name is Mrs. Lee. . . ."

The class giggled.

Mrs. Lee, however, nodded and said, "All right. I guess that's fair. I'll give an oral report about myself, too, Candy. In fact, I'll go first. Let's start on Friday afternoon. That will give you a few days to think about what you want to say."

After school, Bobby and Shawn walked home together. They didn't talk much.

Finally Shawn suggested, "Maybe we should practice."

"Practice what?" Bobby asked.

"Our reports. We could try them out on each other," Shawn said.

Bobby thought about that. "Okay, that's a good idea."

Giving his report to Shawn wouldn't be the same as getting up in front of the class. It would be much, much easier. Shawn was right, though. Practice couldn't hurt.

"Is Lucy ready for the Pet-O-Rama contest?" Shawn asked, changing the subject. "It's this Saturday."

"I know." Bobby didn't want to admit it, but Lucy wasn't quite ready. He had to have a photograph of the pet along with the entry form. His father had tried to take a picture of Lucy, but she wouldn't sit still. So far, the only picture they had was of Lucy's backside as she ran away. Bobby hoped Lucy wasn't getting too wild to be the Pet-O-Rama spokespet.

The boys came to Shawn's front door. "Twitch is all ready to go," Shawn told Bobby. "I've got the cutest picture of him to bring. He's standing up in his cage. He looks like he's smiling."

Bobby sighed. It probably wasn't too hard to take a picture of a little mouse who had nowhere to run.

"How was school today?" Mrs. Quinn asked when Bobby walked into the house.

"Okay," Bobby said.

As soon as Lucy heard Bobby's voice, she came bounding out of the television room.

Bobby leaned down to give her a pat. "Hi, girl," he said. He took her leash off its hook.

"Bobby, you don't sound like things at school are okay," his mother said.

How did his mother always know when

something was wrong? Bobby wondered.

"Can I walk with you and Lucy?" Mrs. Quinn asked.

"Sure." Bobby shrugged. They were hardly out the front gate when Bobby spoke up. "I have to give a report on Friday. I have to talk about myself."

His mother put her arm around Bobby's shoulders. "I know that seems hard for you, Bobby. But you're not as shy as you used to be."

It was true. He talked to Shawn and Candy. He even talked to some of the kids in his class now. That didn't mean he could stand up and talk in front of twenty-five students and one teacher, though.

His dad was wrong. This wasn't going to be such a great year after all.

# The Dreaded Oral Report

"Lucy, look over here." Bobby had his dad's camera. He was trying to take Lucy's picture for the contest on Saturday.

Lucy was curled up on the couch. Mrs. Quinn didn't like Lucy sitting on it. Bobby knew he should shoo her off, but this was the best chance he'd had for a photo all afternoon. When he saw Lucy sitting still for once, Bobby had run upstairs to get the camera. It was a new one, a Father's Day gift from Bobby and his mother. Mr. Quinn had shown Bobby how to use it once or twice.

Lucy tilted her head, watching Bobby. Meanwhile, Bobby fumbled with the camera.

Lucy looked at Bobby for a few seconds longer. Just as he found the right button to push, Lucy jumped off the couch. Bobby checked the screen. He had taken a picture of the pillow Lucy had been lying against.

"Oh, Lucy," Bobby groaned.

Bobby grabbed his notebook and went out to his patio. Lucy was right behind him. Shawn was coming over. They were going to practice their oral reports. Bobby had just sat down when his mother stuck her head out the door. "Visitors, Bobby," she said.

Instead of Shawn and Twitch, out came Candy and Butch.

"Hey, Bobby," Candy said. "Butch and I were taking a walk, and we decided to come see you and Lucy."

Candy bounced across the patio. Butch walked as he usually did—slowly.

Candy saw the camera on the patio table. "Are you taking pictures?" she asked.

"I'm trying to get one of Lucy to bring to the contest on Saturday," Bobby told her. "She keeps running away, though."

"I took a couple of pictures of Butch," Candy said. "I had a different problem. He was asleep in every one of them." Candy sighed. "So, are you and Shawn doing something special this afternoon?"

"We're going to practice our oral reports," Bobby mumbled. He didn't want to talk about it.

Candy was surprised. "How come? I

mean, they're not even real reports. You just have to say a couple of things about yourself. I probably won't even have enough time to say all the things I want to say."

*I bet you won't,* Bobby thought. "Well, uh, Shawn and me, we just don't like getting up to talk."

Candy nodded. "Yeah, my dad had to give a big speech at a company dinner one time. He told me he was scared to death."

"I get that," Bobby replied. If only he had something interesting to say. That might help.

"Hi, guys." Shawn came out to the patio. He was carrying Twitch in his cage. "Hey, it's a regular pet contest out here."

"This might be the only contest Lucy goes to," Bobby said gloomily. "She just won't sit still for her picture."

"And Butch won't stay awake long enough for me to get a good shot of him," Candy added.

Shawn put Twitch down on the patio ledge. He looked at Candy a little nervously. "Are we still going to practice, Bobby?" he asked.

"I guess so." Bobby didn't really want to practice in front of Candy. But if he couldn't give a simple speech in front of her, how could he get up in front of the class? "You can start," he told Shawn politely.

"No, that's all right. You go ahead," said Shawn.

Just then, Candy noticed something. "Look. Look at the dogs and Twitch."

Shawn and Bobby turned and saw what Candy was seeing. Both Lucy and Butch were staring at Twitch in his cage. They

seemed spellbound by the mouse running on his little wheel.

"I've never seen Butch so interested in anything," Candy said.

"Lucy hardly ever stays still for so long anymore," Bobby said.

"Hey . . . ," Candy began.

Bobby picked up on her thought. "I know what you're thinking," he said. "I've got the camera right here."

"Can I go first?" Candy asked.

"Yeah. Lucy's been jumpy lately, I don't want to scare her away," Bobby replied.

"Butch barely moves," Candy said. "But at least he's awake now."

Butch certainly was awake. He couldn't keep his eyes off Twitch.

Candy whispered, "Here, Butch. Look at me." And he did turn his head long enough for Candy to take his picture. She handed the camera to Bobby. "Your turn."

Bobby knew that Lucy would be trickier. She might run away when she saw the camera. Then he had an idea. "Shawn, pick up Twitch's cage. Slowly," he said.

Shawn did what Bobby asked. Lucy got an intense look on her face. It was as if she were saying, *Hey, where's that thing going?* Bobby got the picture.

"Let's download the pictures on the computer. We can see what they look like," Candy suggested.

The kids downloaded the pictures and printed them out. Then it was time for Shawn and Candy to go home.

"Thanks, Bobby. This is a great picture," Candy said as she snapped on Butch's leash.

It *was* a nice picture. Butch looked wide-awake. The photo of Lucy was even better. She had a cute, curious expression. It would be a good picture to bring to the contest.

After Candy left, Shawn said to Bobby, "That was fun. Still, we didn't get to practice our oral reports."

"I know. We'll just have to wing it," Bobby told him. That's what Bobby heard his father say sometimes. Usually it was when Mr. Quinn was worried about not being ready for a business meeting.

*Winging it* had a nice sound, like you'd be flying in the air with no worries or cares. That was not how Bobby felt the next day, however. He felt like he had the weight of the world on his shoulders.

Bobby could hardly keep his mind on anything except the report. He didn't hear

Mrs. Lee call him to the chalkboard during math. During silent reading, he stared out the window. He kept wondering what it would be like to stand at the front of the room, all alone.

Right after lunch, Mrs. Lee leaned against her desk. "I'm so excited about our oral reports today," she said. "I'm eager to learn more about every one of you. And Candy, I'm so glad you had the idea for me to give a report, too. I'll go first, so you can all see about how long I want you to speak."

Mrs. Lee's report on herself held Bobby's attention. He learned that her husband's name was Keir and that she had a teenage son. Her hobbies were scuba diving and knitting—though not at the same time.

Then it was Dexter's turn. Next came Shannon, and after her Candy was up.

Candy's report went on so long that Mrs. Lee had to say, "Fascinating, Candy. But we have to make sure we have time for all the reports."

Then came the moment Bobby had been dreading. Mrs. Lee called his name.

Mrs. Lee had said they didn't need notes, but Bobby wished he had a piece of paper in his hand. It would give him something to hold on to.

Stepping in front of Mrs. Lee's desk, he heard his heart pounding. He wondered if the other kids could hear it, too. *Thump! Thump!* For a few seconds—seconds that seemed like hours—he didn't say a word.

"Bobby, you can start now," Mrs. Lee prompted.

Bobby looked at his classmates. He felt his face getting red. He put his hands behind his back because they were shaking. "Uh, my name is Bobby Quinn. . . ."

"Speak up, Bobby," Mrs. Lee said.

"My name is Bobby Quinn—"

Before Bobby could say another word, an alarm bell started blaring.

Fire drill!

"All right, children," Mrs. Lee said, "this is our first fire drill. Line up quickly and quietly and follow me outside. We'll get back to the reports next week."

Bobby fell into line behind Shawn. He leaned over to whisper to him, "Saved by the bell!"

# Contest Day

The big day was here. The Pet-O-Rama spokespet contest was just a couple of hours away.

Bobby was excited, but he didn't want Lucy to get excited. He wanted her to be calm and cool. He took her aside and told her so. "Lucy, you're going to be in a contest today. There are going to be a lot of other animals there."

Lucy looked interested.

"You'll probably have to parade in front of some judges," Bobby went on. "You can't get crazy. You have to calm down. Okay?"

Lucy snuggled her head under Bobby's hand. Did she understand what Bobby was saying?

Bobby wasn't absolutely sure, but maybe she did. At least when Lucy jumped off the bed where they had been having their chat, she did so slowly. She didn't dash out of the room, knocking things over on the way, either.

Mr. Quinn was going to drive Bobby and Lucy to the contest. Shawn and Twitch were coming with them. Candy and Butch were going to meet them at Pet-O-Rama.

Later that morning, the boys and animals piled into the car. "I wish I could come,"

Mrs. Quinn said. Today was her day to volunteer at the hospital.

"Lucy will bring you back a blue ribbon," Mr. Quinn said.

Shawn frowned.

"Or maybe it will be Twitch," Mr. Quinn added.

"Have a fun time. Lucy, be good," Mrs. Quinn said as the car drove away.

"Do you think there will be a lot of animals at the contest?" Shawn asked.

That question was answered when the car pulled into the mall parking lot in front of Pet-O-Rama. People were walking into the store with dogs, cats, and birds. One person had a ferret.

Lucy put her paws on the open window and looked out. She had never seen so many animals in one place at one time. Her nose wiggled. When they got out of the car, she tugged on her leash to get to the store faster.

"Lucy . . . ," Mr. Quinn said warningly.

Lucy hopped around.

Pet-O-Rama was a madhouse. Barks, meows, squeaks, and chirps came from all directions. Employees in bright red Pet-O-Rama aprons were checking in the pets, getting the photographs from their owners, and then leading people and animals through the back doors.

Outside was a large grassy area, decorated with colorful balloons. Along the fence were a table and chairs for the judges. Altogether there were about thirty furry, feathered, or scaly contestants.

"Hey, Bobby, Shawn! Over here." Candy and her mother were standing next to Butch. Despite the hubbub, he was taking a nap.

While the grown-ups talked, Candy said, "Guess who's here?"

"Who?" Bobby asked.

"Mrs. Agatha Adams and her cat, Ginger," Candy told them.

"Uh-oh!" Bobby said. Over the summer he and Shawn had spent one long afternoon trying to find Lucy when she was chasing Ginger all over town.

Lucy gave a happy yip when she saw Ginger. She pulled at her leash as if she wanted to start chasing Ginger all over again.

Ginger, however, gave Lucy a disdainful look. She turned away from the beagle, her tail up in the air.

"Ginger looks pretty today," Candy said.

"Her collar makes her look like a queen."

"She's not as cute as Twitch," Shawn said loyally.

"She's not as cute as Lucy, either," Bobby said.

Candy looked down at the drooling Butch. He was snoring. "She's probably cuter than Butch." Candy was very honest. She added, "There are plenty of cute pets here."

Just then, a woman with lots of brown hair piled on top of her head blew a silver whistle. Everyone stopped talking and paid attention.

"Pets and pet owners, welcome. I am Lydia Jones, the manager of this Pet-O-Rama. In a few moments our contest will start. As you know, the winner gets free pet food for a year. Our winner will also go on to compete with the winners from the other Pet-O-Rama stores throughout the state."

The crowd buzzed.

Ms. Jones blew on her whistle again. "I would like everyone to line up with their pets. Then you and your pet will walk past the judges' table."

Ms. Jones introduced them. One worked at Pet-O-Rama. He looked important. Another was a dog trainer. The third was the editor of the local newspaper.

There was a bit of a rush to line up. Bobby was worried that Lucy wouldn't like all the confusion, but she took it in stride. In fact, she seemed to like being in the middle of all the hubbub.

An accordion player began a lively tune. Ms. Jones gave the go-ahead, and the animals and their owners started parading in front of the judges. A photographer from the paper snapped pictures as the pets marched by.

Bobby, Shawn, and Candy were in the middle of the line. It was moving a little slowly. One of their dogs was getting restless and started barking. Then that dog tried to race to the front of the line. But it wasn't Lucy. It was Butch.

"Butch, cool it," Candy said. She must have said it five times.

Butch, however, wasn't in the mood to cool it. Instead he stood in front of the judges' table, barking. That got some of the other dogs in the contest barking, too. Candy tried to pull him back in line.

Ms. Jones came over to Candy and whispered in her ear. Candy looked sad, but she nodded. She walked Butch over to her mom, who gave her a hug.

"Wow," Shawn said. "Candy and Butch got kicked out of the contest."

Bobby shook his head. "What a time for Butch finally to get excited about something." He glanced down at Lucy. She seemed as cool as a cucumber. When she got to the front of the line, she strolled slowly past the judges. The photographer kneeled down to get a picture of Lucy. She stopped and posed for him. Bobby was surprised. What a time for Lucy to calm down!

All the other animals marched past the judges. Then Ms. Jones said, "We have cake and punch for you and treats for the pets. Please enjoy them while the judges make their decision."

Bobby, Shawn, and Candy ate cake and waited for the judges. Bobby thought Candy would be upset about Butch, but nothing

bothered her for long. "At least I got some cake out of the deal," she said.

Bobby looked over at the judges. They were going through the animals' pictures and talking. Bobby wished he were close enough to hear them.

He kneeled down next to his dog. "Whether you win or lose, Lucy, you did good," he said. Lucy licked Bobby's cheek. Maybe she was just licking off some frosting that had landed there, but Bobby didn't think so.

Finally Ms. Jones went to the microphone. She had a piece of paper and a photograph in her hand. "Our winner is the little beagle, Lucy Quinn."

Lucy! Bobby jumped up and gave a whoop. Lucy won. This was absolutely the best news ever!

# Uh-oh!

This was absolutely the worst news ever!

Everything was fine when Lucy had won her blue ribbon. And when the photographer took lots of pictures for the newspaper. And when everyone congratulated Bobby and Lucy. Then Ms. Jones pulled Bobby, Lucy, and Mr. Quinn aside.

"Now, you understand that the finals for the Pet-O-Rama spokespet contest are next week in the state capital," Ms. Jones said.

"Yes, we know," Mr. Quinn answered. "We'll be there."

"Good, good." Ms. Jones beamed at Lucy. "I think our little beagle has a good chance of winning the whole thing. She's delightful."

Lucy quietly basked in the praise. Clearly, she didn't mind being described as delightful.

"If Lucy wins the contest, it will be a big opportunity for you, too, Bobby," Ms. Jones went on. "If she becomes the Pet-O-Rama spokespet, she will be in several television commercials."

Mr. Quinn nodded. "I remember that was on the entry form."

"The pet's owner is part of the commercials as well. I'm sure Pet-O-Rama would like to feature a boy and his dog." Ms. Jones beamed down at Bobby.

Bobby looked up at his father in horror. Before he or his father could say anything, Ms. Jones was pulled away by one of her employees.

"I can't be in a commercial," Bobby said.

"I know it wouldn't be your favorite thing, Bobby," his father said. "But you might not have many lines. It could be fun."

Bobby thought about being in a TV studio with lots of strange adults telling him what to say and how to act. A scared, nervous feeling ran through his body. He looked at his father and shook his head.

"We're getting a little ahead of ourselves, Bobby," his dad added. "Lucy might not win that contest. For now, let's enjoy Lucy's win today."

That's what Bobby tried to do. Lucy was certainly enjoying it. If she were a cat, she would have purred. Instead she gave short, happy barks when anyone petted her.

Bobby's mother was home when they got back. She saw Lucy's blue ribbon right away. "Lucy won!" she exclaimed. "Tell me all about it."

So Bobby and his dad sat around the kitchen table and gave Mrs. Quinn a blow-by-blow account. Bobby got excited all over again about Lucy's win. Then Mr. Quinn explained about the television commercials, and Bobby felt himself flatten like a popped balloon.

"How do you feel about being in a commercial, Bobby?" his mom asked.

"Not good," Bobby muttered.

"Would you do it?" Mrs. Quinn wanted to know.

Bobby hung his head. "I don't think I could."

Mr. and Mrs. Quinn looked at each other. Mrs. Quinn said, "If you don't want to do it, I'm not sure it would be fair to let Lucy take part in the contest."

Bobby looked up, shocked.

Mr. Quinn explained, "Pet-O-Rama is counting on a winner and an owner to be in the commercials."

"You could be in it, Dad. Or you, Mom."

"I think the company would rather have a boy," his father replied. "Besides, Lucy is your dog."

Bobby felt terrible. He didn't want to keep Lucy from her big chance. But he didn't want to be in a commercial, either.

Mrs. Quinn looked at Bobby. "Bobby, we have a couple of days to think about this. Let's not make any decisions right now. Okay?"

"Okay," Bobby agreed.

"In the meantime, let's hang the blue ribbon on the living room mirror," she said.

That night when Bobby was getting under his covers, Lucy jumped up on his bed like she always did. Bobby gave her a big hug. "You had a good time today, huh, Lucy?"

Lucy wriggled closer to Bobby.

"You'd have a good time in the contest next week, too," Bobby said.

Lucy just looked at Bobby with her big brown eyes.

"You could win that contest. You could be the Pet-O-Rama spokespet, easy." Bobby flopped back against his pillow. This was Lucy's big chance. Was it going to be ruined all because of him?

# Starring Lucy and Bobby

Now Bobby had two worries. He still had to stand in front of the class and give his oral report. And he had to decide what to do about the contest.

On Monday at school, it was time to deal with Worry #1. Mrs. Lee said, "I'm sorry the fire drill interrupted our oral reports. We'll get back to them later today."

All morning Bobby worried. He worried

through math and he worried through spelling. It was raining hard during recess, so the class stayed inside. Mrs. Lee read from *The Mouse and the Motorcycle.* Bobby barely heard her, and he loved that book.

Soon it was almost lunchtime. Maybe he wouldn't have to give his report until the afternoon. Then he had an even better thought. Maybe Mrs. Lee would forget it was his turn. Or what if she thought he had finished his report before the fire-drill bell rang? That would be great!

But at eleven forty-five, Mrs. Lee said, "Let's get to some reports."

Mrs. Lee looked around the room. Bobby held his breath. Then her eyes landed right on him. "I think you were speaking when the bell rang, right, Bobby?"

"Yes, ma'am," he whispered. Bobby

dragged himself to the front of the room.

"All right, Bobby. Start over, and speak up nice and loud," Mrs. Lee said.

Bobby looked at all his classmates looking back at him. He felt a little dizzy. He fixed his eyes on the clock at the back of the room. "My name is Bobby Quinn. I live with my parents. I like to draw superheroes. . . ." Bobby rushed along. "And I have a beagle named Lucy. I got her this summer for my birthday. Any questions?"

That was how Mrs. Lee told them to end their reports, by asking if the class had any questions. Hoping there weren't any, Bobby turned to go back to his seat.

"Bobby," a familiar voice called.

Oh no! Candy had raised her hand. Bobby frowned. Some friend.

"Bobby, you should tell the class about

how Lucy won the contest on Saturday," Candy said.

Bobby could feel his face getting hot. That was a long story.

"Did Lucy win that contest at Pet-O-Rama?" Mrs. Lee asked.

Bobby nodded.

"I almost entered my kitten in that contest. Tell us about it," Mrs. Lee said.

"Well . . . ," Bobby shyly began, "the contest was out behind the Pet-O-Rama store. I came with Lucy. Shawn brought his mouse, Twitch."

"I was there, too," Candy said, waving her hand. "With my dog, Butch."

"Yes, Butch was there." Bobby didn't mention the trouble Butch had caused.

"Was there lots going on?" Mrs. Lee asked.

"There was pretty good food, and music, and balloons, and stuff."

"What kind of pets were there?" Dexter called from his seat.

"Dogs, cats, even a ferret," Bobby remembered. "The judges thought Lucy was the best." For the first time during his report, Bobby smiled.

"What did she win?" Grace asked.

"A blue ribbon. And some free dog food," Bobby said.

"Don't forget she's got a chance to be the

Pet-O-Rama spokespet," Shawn reminded him.

"What's a spokespet?" one of the kids wanted to know.

Bobby explained about the next contest. He felt a little knot in his stomach when he talked about the television commercials. The other kids thought it would be great to be in a commercial.

"Television! That would be awesome," Dexter said. "You and Lucy would rock!"

Everyone in the class seemed to agree.

"Well, thank you, Bobby. That report was wonderful," Mrs. Lee said. "We'll all be eager to hear if Lucy wins the next contest."

Bobby went back to his seat. Grace got up to give her report. But Bobby was thinking about what had just happened. He had been very, very nervous when he started speaking. Then everyone was so interested in Lucy and the contest. Talking to his classmates had seemed easy. He couldn't quite believe it.

When Bobby got home from school, he and his mom took Lucy for her walk. He told her what had happened.

Mrs. Quinn pulled her sweater around her. It was getting cold. "Well, Bobby, you were talking about something interesting and exciting. The other kids thought it was interesting and exciting, too."

"I was talking about Lucy," Bobby said.

Lucy heard her name and turned around.

"Everyone likes hearing about Lucy," Bobby added.

"So have you thought any more about the contest?" Mrs. Quinn asked.

Bobby nodded. "I think we should go."

"Are you sure?"

"Yes," Bobby said. "This is a big chance for Lucy. I don't want to spoil it for her. She likes to be the center of attention. I don't. But today, it wasn't too bad. I think I could be in those commercials if Lucy wins."

Mrs. Quinn gave Bobby a hug. "You're getting so brave, Bobby."

Lucy barked. She agreed.

# And the Winner Is . . .

"Wow!" Bobby said. He looked around the park. It was across from the state capitol building.

Everything here was bigger and better than the contest at the mall. Candy-colored Pet-O-Rama banners decorated the park. Instead of an accordion player, there was a band. A television crew was taping the event. Even the animals were different.

"These guys look like they belong in a zoo, not a pet store," Mr. Quinn said.

A couple of cats and dogs were there, but they were the fancy kind, like the fluffy white Persian kitten in her owner's arms.

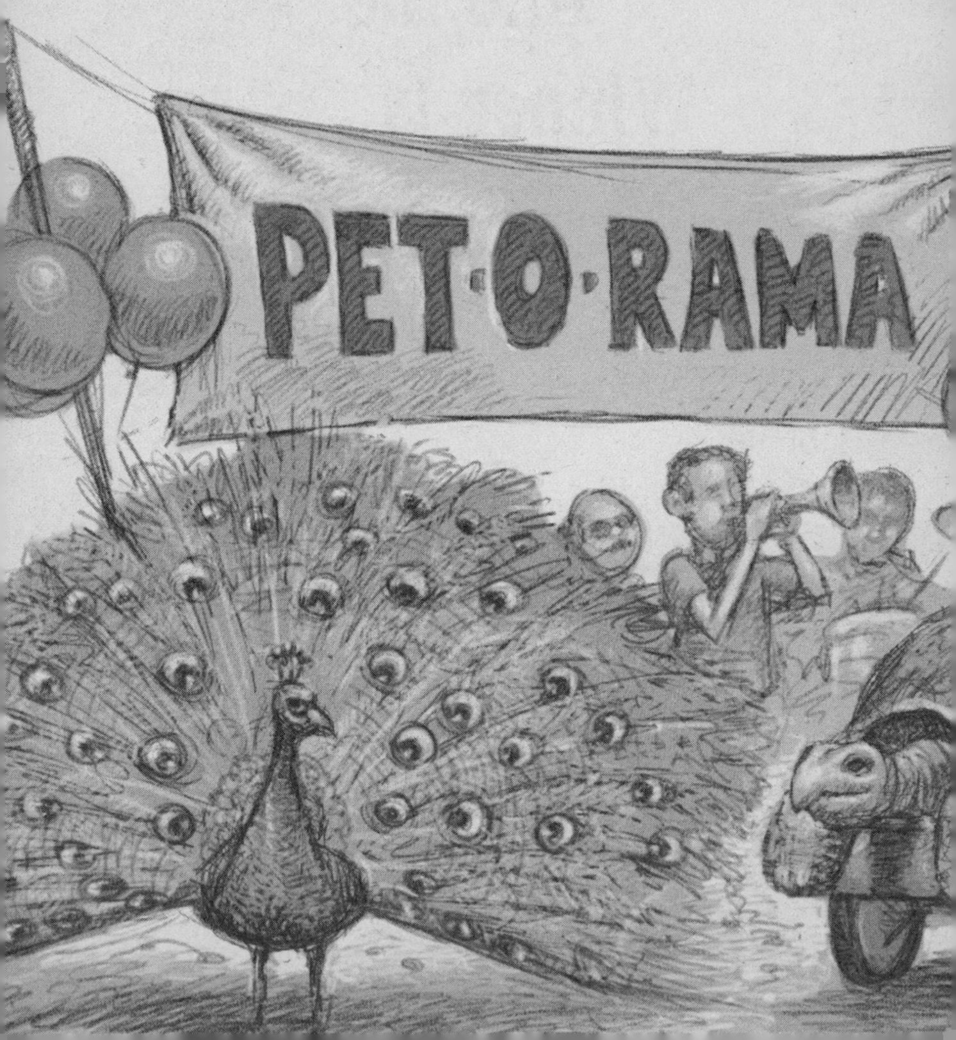

There were also more exotic pets. One turtle was so big he had to be pulled in a wagon. A large green and blue parrot rested on someone's arm. Bobby spied something even more colorful. "Look!"

A peacock next to an older lady spread its fan of beautiful blue and green feathers. Lucy seemed stunned at the display. She didn't even bark.

"Lions and tigers and bears. Oh my," Mr. Quinn said.

There weren't any lions or tigers or bears around. Bobby knew that was just a line from the movie *The Wizard of Oz*.

Bobby whispered to Lucy, "You're cuter than any of these animals." He was still nervous about being in a TV commercial, but he also still thought Lucy should win.

Before very long, Bobby and Lucy were given a number. The woman in charge of the contest lined up all the pets and owners. Bobby and Lucy were behind the turtle. They were in front of the parrot.

Each pet and owner stopped and talked

to the judges. The judges asked lots of questions. They looked at the animals carefully. It took a long time.

Lucy was getting bored. When she got bored, she got jumpy. She started pulling toward the white kitten, which was behind the parrot. Bobby wondered if the cat reminded her of Mrs. Agatha Adams's cat, Ginger.

"Calm down, Lucy," Bobby said. "No cat chasing today. Please."

Finally it was Lucy's turn.

"Hello," said a judge with gray hair. His name tag said, GREG SMITH, PRESIDENT, PET-O-RAMA.

Bobby gulped. He had never talked to a president before.

"Tell us about Lucy," Mr. Smith said.

"Lucy's the best dog ever," Bobby began softly. Then he remembered to speak up like when he gave his report. Bobby tried to talk more loudly.

He told the judge how he got Lucy for his birthday, and how she was his best friend.

A lady judge asked Bobby, "Would you enjoy being in a television commercial, Bobby?"

*Enjoy?* "Ah, I think Lucy would like it," he answered honestly.

The judges spent a lot of time looking at Lucy. Lucy did her little prancy dance.

The lady judge thanked Bobby. He and Lucy were about to move on when he heard a squawk behind him. "PET-O-RAMA! RWWK! PET-O-RAMA!"

Bobby whirled around. It was the parrot. Lucy let loose with a howl, but Bobby could see the judges' eyes light up with interest.

"I think I know who the winner is going

to be," Mrs. Quinn said. She was waiting for Bobby at the end of the line.

She didn't mean Lucy.

Sure enough, when the judges named the winner, it was Poll the Parrot.

"She is very beautiful," Mr. Smith said. He added happily, "And she can tell people to shop at Pet-O-Rama in her own special way."

Bobby and his parents got ready to go back home.

"I'm sorry you didn't win, Lucy," Bobby said when they were in the car.

"It's hard to beat a parrot that's squawking 'Pet-O-Rama,' " Mr. Quinn said.

Lucy didn't seem to mind. She was chomping on a big bone-shaped biscuit the Pet-O-Rama lady had given to all the dog contestants.

Bobby thought about the band and the banners, the parrot and the peacock. And that giant turtle. "I still have a lot to tell the class," Bobby said, grinning.

"You're looking forward to giving a report about it?" Mrs. Quinn asked, a little surprised.

Bobby was a little surprised himself. Standing in front of the class didn't seem so hard anymore. He was excited about it. "Yes, I am." He gave Lucy a big hug. "Absolutely."

**Read all the books about Bobby and Lucy!**

# Absolutely Lucy

Bobby's mother smiled. "Now it's time for your special present," she said.

His father said, "Close your eyes."

Bobby was glad to close his eyes. It would be easier to look surprised when he opened them.

"Okay, Bobby," his father called, "you can look!"

Bobby opened his eyes. He didn't have to pretend to be surprised. Or happy. In his father's arms was a puppy. The cutest, squirmiest little dog Bobby had ever seen.

# Lucy on the Loose

"Ben!" Shawn said. "What happened to Lucy?"

"She . . . she ran away!" Ben said in a shaky voice.

Bobby jumped up. "Ran away? Where?"

"That way." Ben was confused. He pointed in one direction. "Or maybe that way." He pointed in the other direction.

"Which way was it?" Shawn demanded.

"I'm not sure." Ben was almost crying. "But she was chasing a big orange C-A-T!"

# About the Author

When Ilene Cooper started thinking about her third Lucy book, she came up with the title first—*Look at Lucy!* Then she had to figure out why everyone was looking at the little beagle. Soon she had the idea that Lucy could be part of a pet contest, but how would Lucy's owner, Bobby, feel about that when he's so shy?

Ilene Cooper is the 2007 winner of the Prairie State Award for her body of work and has written more than twenty-five books for children, including *The Golden Rule,* which won a gold recommendation from *Parents* magazine; and *Jack: The Early Years of John F. Kennedy,* an American Library Association Notable Children's Book. Of course, she also wrote the first two books about Bobby and Lucy, *Absolutely Lucy* and *Lucy on the Loose.*